WHO'S BACK AT THE DOOR?

JC BRATTON

BLUE MILK Publishing

Who's Back at the Door?

By JC Bratton

Copyright © 2023 by JC Bratton

ISBN-13: 978-1-7367715-1-8 (paperback)

ISBN-13: 978-1-7367715-2-5 (e-book)

Library of Congress Control Number: 2023916196

First printing, October 2023

Blue Milk Publishing: San Jose, California

PROLOGUE

The Ohio State University Campus
October 3, 2017

"So, Jamie and Mark got back together — again."

Shelly Patel rolled her eyes as she took a sip of her latte. Chatter filled a campus Starbucks, but Shelly and her friend Steve were still able to make conversation.

"I still don't understand what Jamie was so upset about. I mean, Mark is like *the* most devoted boyfriend *ever*." Shelly's tone was a bit somber.

"Do I sense a bit of jealousy?" Steve asked as he ate his croissant.

"No, no. Jamie is my girl. Chicks before di—" Before Shelly could complete her sentence, a loud crackle of thunder sounded.

"Shoot, I need to get back." Shelly jumped out of her chair and picked up her backpack.

"I'll see you tonight?" Shelly asked Steve.

"Of course!" Steve gave Shelly a warm smile as she headed out.

———

Shelly ran back to her North Campus dorm before it started to rain. She needed to get ready for rush events followed by a huge party at the Tri-Delta house. Steve acted as Shelly's "plus one," a role he played since high school. She hoped that Jamie would still be available, as it was critical for Shelly to get Jamie's opinion about the dress she planned to wear at the party. To make matters worse, her phone died, so she desperately needed her charger.

It was a little past 3:30 PM, and the dorm hallway was dimly lit. There were periodic rumbles from the thunderstorm brewing outside. As Shelly approached room 1138, something didn't seem right. The door was slightly open.

"That's odd," Shelly muttered. She then slowly pushed the door. "Jamie?"

There was someone in the room, but it was not Jamie. It was a woman with long dark hair covering her face and pale skin. She wore a white gown. The woman turned straight to Shelly and growled.

Shelly screamed in terror and ran as fast as she could down the hallway. The lights began to flicker, and Shelly could still hear the growling from the woman, as if she was following her. Not turning her back to see, Shelly quickly ran down the staircase and opened the door to the first floor. On the other side of the door was Tabitha, a Resident Advisor for the dorm.

"Help!" Shelly yelled. "She's after me!"

"Who? Who's after you?" Tabitha questioned and looked around and up the staircase. "Um, there is no one here. Look."

Panting, Shelly hesitated and then turned around to see an empty staircase. Suddenly, there were footsteps. Shelly screamed!

"Hey, I'm not that scary!" Tom Doyle, a Freshman,

remarked in a sarcastic tone as he waved his hands up in the air and proceeded down the staircase.

"What is your name?" Tabitha asked.

"Shelly. Shelly Patel from room 1138."

"Okay, Shelly. What exactly happened?"

Shelly took a deep breath and explained the situation to Tabitha.

"I room with my friend Jamie. The door was slightly open, and I saw a woman with dark hair and a white gown. She began growling at me. It frightened me, and I ran down the stairs."

"You have no idea who this woman is?" Tabitha asked.

"Not in the slightest. Also, I didn't see Jamie. I hope she is okay! My phone is dead. I have no idea if she's been trying to call me." Shelly took out her phone and stared at a blank, life-less screen.

"Well, Shelly, let's head to the campus police station and see if they can help."

———

"No, Mrs. Wilson," the male officer explained. "It's rush week. That naked boy in your yard wasn't trying to invade your home." Officer Julian couldn't help but snicker as she overheard her colleague on the phone. As the conversation continued, Shelly and Tabitha entered the office.

"Hey, Tabitha!" Officer Julian smiled as she recognized the RA. "What's going on?"

"My name is Shelly Patel," Shelly interjected before Tabitha could speak. "I live at Swift Tower, room 1138, with my roommate, Jamie Patterson. There was a strange woman who was in our room. She had long, dark hair and wore a white gown…"

Officer Julian's colleague immediately hung up the phone and gave Shelly an inquisitive look.

"A woman in white?" he asked. Shelly nodded nervously in agreement.

"I'm Officer Scott. So, your roommate's name is Jamie Patterson? Long dark hair? Her boyfriend is Mark Stevens?" Shelly and Tabitha looked at each other in amazement as Officer Scott spoke those words.

"I used to work for the County Sheriff. I had a, uh, mishap that involved Jamie and Mark this past summer. It led me to my 'demotion' and assignment here at campus police." Officer Scott rolled his eyes.

"So, can you help us, Officer Scott?" Shelly asked anxiously.

Officer Scott pulled up Shelly and Jamie's records on his computer.

"You're at Swift Tower? We have some surveillance cameras. Officer Julian can look through the last 24 hours of footage. While she does that, let's head back to the room. Who knows? Jamie may be back as well."

———

It was close to 6 PM, and the storm had passed. Shelly, Tabitha, and Officer Scott walked down the hallway to the dorm room. The door was wide open.

"Wait here," Officer Scott commanded. He walked through the suite, checked each door, looked under each bed, checked the lounge, the bathroom… no sign of anyone.

"Well?" Tabitha asked. "Is the coast clear?"

"Yeah, come in!" Officer Scott shouted.

Shelly found her charging cable and was able to glance at her messages. There was a text from Jamie at 3 PM:

Shell, I am heading to the library this afternoon. I hope to be back by 5.

"Oh no!" Shelly exclaimed. "Jamie's text says she should have been back by 5. It's 6 PM!"

Officer Scott's phone rang; it was Officer Julian. He placed her on speaker phone.

"Hey, Julian, what did you find?"

"Ummm — you've got to see this in person. You all should get back down here *now!*"

————

The group headed back to the campus police station and found Officer Julian studying the camera footage on her computer.

"Hey, this is super weird," Officer Julian explained. "As you can see here, at 3:33 PM, the door to room 1138 suddenly opens, as if on its own. Then, around 3:35, we see Shelly enter in and then run out of the room and down the hall — but then look what happens. Shelly, based on what you claimed, there should be a 'woman in white' following you. That's not the case."

"Oh my God!" Shelly shouted. "That's... that's Jamie!"

————

Clipping from *The Columbus Dispatch*, October 20, 2017

Information wanted on the whereabouts of Jamie Ann Patterson, 18, who has been missing since October 3rd. She was last seen leaving her dorm at Swift Tower on the OSU campus. Her room-mate, Shelly Lynn Patel, 18, witnessed a mysterious woman present at the time Jamie was last seen. The only sign of potential vandalism was Ms. Patel's mirror; it was found with a large crack running diagonally through it...

CHAPTER 1

Present Day

J amie was gone. After seven years, Mark finally accepted that fact. Even with the video footage from Swift Tower, Shelly's testimony, and *everything* Mark had witnessed, the idea that "Bloody Mary," a childhood urban legend, was behind Jamie's disappearance didn't sit well with the authorities. In fact, the Waverly County Sheriff's office, the department that *knew* Bloody Mary was real, would not assist.

"This case is not in my jurisdiction, young Mark," Sheriff King said sympathetically. "I'm sorry that Miss Jamie is missing, but my hands are tied."

Even Jamie's parents were skeptical. With the video footage showing Jamie leaving on her own, and the fact that many young women go missing, they felt it had to have been an abduction. The local television show *Missing* released an episode on November 18, 2017, that discussed the "facts" of Jamie's disappearance and featured Mr. and Mrs. Patterson.

"Jamie is our baby." Mr. Patterson spoke directly to the camera while tears rolled down his face. "We… we need her back home safely. If you know *anything* about our Jamie, please contact the authorities. We *beg* of you."

There was no mention of Shelly's encounter with The Woman in White, and no one dared to bring up Bloody Mary.

Things That Go Bump in the Night radio and podcast host Pete Williams, however, suspected it was Bloody Mary all along. There had been an influx of supernatural or paranormal events since the death of Dr. Scott Collier, the scientist from MIT who may have inadvertently opened a portal to another dimension — one in which urban legends were real.

"Mark," Pete said in a serious tone over the phone one night. "I am receiving reports of very unusual phenomena: a man in a fedora haunting people in their sleep, a set of Japanese dolls that are possessed, mobile apps that know when you are going to die… yet, the authorities just want to bury this. When science and convention offer us no answers, might we not finally turn to the fantastic as a possible explanation?"

Rather than focusing on his schoolwork and internship with the Jet Propulsion Lab at Caltech, Mark spent most of his time chasing leads with Pete. It led to Mark's academic suspension after his Sophomore year. Although Mark's parents were not happy about him ignoring his college education, they did their best to support their son and helped fund his travels with Pete. But, after seven years of "wild goose chases," even Mark's parents had enough.

"Mark, we know how much Jamie meant to you, but it's really time to move on," Mark's mom said in a firm tone. "These 'investigations' with Pete *have to stop*. Look, we worked it out with Jamie's dad. He is willing to give you a job at Patterson AI. But, this 'Bloody Mary' business has to stop. *Now.*"

Mark thought it over. Maybe they were all right; maybe it was just time to move on? Shelly worked at Patterson AI in the procurement department. She adjusted back to normalcy. In fact, she blew up at Mark about five years prior.

"Mark, I just can't anymore," Shelly said in a serious tone. "Yes, I think I saw *something* in the dorm hallway that night, but I am sick and tired of you and Pete bugging me for more details. There is nothing more I can offer you. Please, Mark, move on or get some professional help."

Could Mark *really* move on? What else could he do? He lost his chance at Caltech, his friends thought he was crazy, and his parents were going to cut him off. He could move to Nevada and crash with Pete. But, for what result? Seven years and no sign of Jamie…

Mark sided with practicality. He took the offer from Jamie's dad. It was a full time engineering role with a great benefits package and stock in the company. A condition of his employment, however, was that he no longer stay in contact with Pete Williams.

"I'm sorry, Pete. It's time for me to just move on," Mark told Pete over the phone.

"But, Mark, we are so close! Dr. Paul Yang, the Silicon Valley parapsychologist, may have a lead for us —"

Mark interrupted Pete. "No! No, Pete. No more leads. I'm just done."

CHAPTER 2

Ross and Mary Montgomery moved to the San Francisco Bay Area shortly after Jamie's disappearance. Ross received a job offer to join a very prestigious Silicon Valley tech firm. Ross, however, would only take the opportunity if he felt Mary could also benefit.

Mary had no issue with moving. In fact, a lot had changed for her. She gained a sense of confidence that she didn't have prior. She grew out of her physically awkward phase and radiated with beauty, both inside and out. Her confidence was also reflected in her school work. She graduated from high school a whole year early. Mary attended UC Berkeley for undergrad and became fascinated with lucid dreaming and parasomnias. Her senior capstone project centered around the research of Dr. Scott Collier and how people may be able to manipulate their dreams.

Dr. Paul Yang, who ran a private sleep clinic in Silicon Valley, near the Stanford campus, was very impressed with Mary's research project. As a result, he invited her to intern with his team for the summer before graduate school commenced at Berkeley in the Fall.

"Oh my God, Mary! I'm so happy for you!" Ross gave Mary a gigantic hug when he read the letter from Dr. Yang.

"Thanks, Dad," Mary said with a smile. "I owe it all to you. Thank you for always believing in me."

"Of course," Ross said with encouragement. "Based on the letter, it looks like you'll have a new place to stay. You never got to experience living on your own. Are you sure you'll be okay with the transition?"

"Well, I just turned 21," Mary assured her dad. "I think it's time that I test the waters. I mean, it's just for the summer. How hard can that be?"

"Looks like you start next week! Wow! Maybe it's time I introduce you to your graduation present?" Ross gave Mary a half-smirk as he led her to the garage…

————

Mary's graduation gift was an all-electric Ioniq. This car aligned perfectly with Mary's values. She wanted not only to help people but also the planet. Mary packed up a few necessities and headed toward the Stanford campus.

It wasn't clear where Mary would be staying. The letter only mentioned "near the Stanford campus." Mary opted to head straight to the sleep clinic and would worry about the details of her stay later.

The sleep clinic had a classic Silicon Valley feel; it reeked of innovation. The windows were large — tons of light — an open architecture that looked unfinished but full of style. Mary entered the reception area only to be immediately greeted by Dr. Paul Yang.

"Mary. Mary Montgomery! I am so excited you decided to intern with us!" Dr. Yang said enthusiastically.

"Oh you cannot believe how thrilled I am, Dr. Yang!" Mary exclaimed. "I decided to drive straight here to the lab rather than to the apartment—"

"First off, call me Paul," Dr. Yang interjected. "And second, did Alex not tell you? You will be living in a gorgeous, recently renovated house! We have some houses that have been allocated to our visiting scholars, and you, dear, are a V.I.P. Let me send a quick text to Alex. You know Alex Anderson, right?"

Mary saw from the clinic's website that she was on the staff as Paul's assistant, but she knew little about her.

"Well, I know *of* her, but I have not met her formally," Mary replied.

"Let me text her now. I was out of town last week, and she was supposed to send you the housing details. Normally Alex is very prompt, so I am not sure why you didn't receive this information with your letter." Paul typed quickly on his mobile phone. "Okay, text sent! Let's get your badge, and then I'll show you where I need your help first."

Paul swiped his badge and opened the big glass door entrance into the main part of the lab.

———

Mary's first task, unfortunately, wasn't one she hoped. Paul assigned her to help sort and file a bunch of papers that came from Dr. Scott Collier's lab at MIT. The boxes sat in the lab for years, but Paul never had the time or patience to go through them all. All the boxes were moved to the third floor — a dimly-lit part of the building in stark contrast to the rest of the modern architecture.

Mary let out a sigh. "Oh well, Mary, all great researchers have to start somewhere." She opened room number three and turned on the light.

The room contained a desk, a chair, some supplies, a filing cabinet, and a laptop. There were at least 50 boxes stacked in the corner; however, one was set aside from the pack. The label on the box read *May 2017*.

"Oh wow, Dr. Collier died that month," Mary said to herself. As a result, the box piqued Mary's curiosity. Mary took a box cutter from the desk and opened it. Large stacks of manila folders filled the box. Maybe something ground-breaking would appear? To Mary's disappointment, folder number one read "Receipts." Mary let out a big sigh, but, as any other eager intern would do, she continued onward.

"This is going to take a while," Mary muttered to herself.

She began organizing each folder into the filing cabinet per Paul's instructions...

CHAPTER 3

A benefit of working on Dr. Yang's team was rent-free living in a gorgeous home near the Stanford campus. Alex Anderson did not take advantage of this perk until recently. She lived with her friend Steph in Mountain View, but then Steph had to move to North Carolina to take care of her elderly mother after her father passed away from Covid. Alex moved into the split-level home only a few weeks prior. The bottom level was to be occupied by Paul's new intern, Mary Montgomery.

As Paul's assistant, Alex had to get the house prepped for Mary's arrival. She also needed to send a message to Mary with the details of her stay.

A visiting scholar from Ohio State occupied the lower level for a few months and left behind a bunch of items, most of which were going to be donated. Alex had a lot of tidying up to do. In addition, a specific request came from Paul himself. He wanted a video doorbell installed as an extra security measure.

"Hey, I have absolutely no idea how to install this thing," Alex confessed to her boyfriend, Mike.

"What? You mean the doorbell camera?" Mike asked.

"Come on, it's a piece of cake! Leave it to me." Mike took out the parts and started assembling the device.

Mike and Alex had been dating on-and-off for the last seven years. After break-up number ten, they seemed to finally get on the same page. Mike planned on crashing a few days a week at the house, although, technically, Alex wasn't allowed to have sleep-over guests due to some line item in the 50-page contract she had to sign. This was the last day Alex would see Mike for at least a few days, as he was slated to work some long shifts at the fire station.

"Oh, shoot. I missed last night's episode of *Things That Go Bump in the Night*, and it featured Paul. I'm going to listen to it, okay, Mike?" Mike didn't even hear Alex, as he was hyper-focused on the installation. Alex put on her headphones and loaded up the latest podcast episode as she began sorting through the first pile of items to be donated.

Pete: Welcome to Things That Go Bump in the Night. Pete Williams here coming to you from the high desert in Nevada. Tonight we have a special guest. It's Dr. Paul Yang, world renowned psychologist and parapsychology enthusiast. Gosh, Dr. Yang, it's been, what, seven years since you appeared on the program? How are you?

Dr. Yang: I'm well, Pete. Very well.

Pete: Good to hear. Doctor, from what I gather you left Stanford to start your own clinic. How has that been going?

Dr. Yang: Very good, Pete. Let me first say that I have no ill-will towards Stanford; they were very supportive. However, I really wanted to branch out to areas that, let's just say, are unconventional. So, it was best for me to separate from Stanford and seek private funding.

Pete: And that's where Patterson AI came in?

Dr. Yang: Exactly. Allan Patterson, the brilliant robotics engineer-turned-entrepreneur, has become heavily interested in sleep and the research of the late Dr. Scott Collier — may he rest in peace.

Pete: I am curious, Dr. Yang, do you know what really happened to Dr. Collier that night in Seattle?

Dr. Yang: Umm, not sure why I am being asked this, but we all know that Scott died in a car accident…

Pete: I hate to tell you, Dr. Yang, but that's not the case. Scott was murdered. And you know the murderer, don't you — ALEX…

Pete Williams's tone changed. It was an eery cackle. It was the man in the fedora!

"No!" Alex screamed.

"Alex, babe! I think you're having a nightmare." Mike reached over to wake Alex, as she appeared to have fallen asleep on the sofa. She held a small package in her hand. Mike moved the package onto the coffee table and sat next to her.

"Mike! It's the man in the fedora… he's *back*!" Alex trembled.

"It was just a dream, Alex. What were you listening to anyway?" Mike looked over at her phone and saw the program name on the screen. "*Things That Go Bump in the Night*? You really need to stop listening to that show."

"Seriously, listen to the episode!" Alex changed her audio source to speaker and began playing the episode for Mike.

Pete: Haha! I'm glad you still have your sense of humor, Dr.

*Yang. I wish you all the best in your research. We'll be back
in a moment and will take your calls for Open Line Friday.*

"Umm, what was I supposed to hear? That's just Pete
Williams…" Mike gave a perplexed look.

"But, that's not…" Alex felt a bit embarrassed. "God, I
guess it really was just a nightmare. How long was I out?"
Alex asked.

"Well, long enough to have a video doorbell installed!
Take a look." Mike tried to lighten the mood. He and Alex
walked over to the front door to see the new video doorbell
installed and ready to go.

"You're a life saver!" Alex gave Mike a hug and a kiss.

"It's what I do!" Mike winked. "I left the instructions on
how to install the app and complete the configuration on the
kitchen counter." Mike looked at his watch. "Ouch! It's 3:30
AM. I have to head to the station now — late shift awaits!"

Alex watched Mike as he entered his car and drove off.
She couldn't shake the nightmare. Something didn't seem
right. Alex closed the door and proceeded back to the living
room. She noticed the package on the coffee table.

"Okay, Alex. No more urban legends. Back to reality —
and junk sorting." She let out a big sigh and grabbed the
package.

Before Alex could open the package, she heard the doorbell ring. Maybe it was Mike? Alex walked to the door and
opened it immediately. No one was there.

Alex then heard a woman's voice. It was muffled and
seemed to say, "Help." Alex left the door open and walked
over to the sofa. The package and her phone were where she
left them. Alex listened carefully and heard the woman's
voice again, but it was much louder this time: "Help!" It came
from inside one of the boxes — a long box that had the word
"mirror" written in red!

"What in the world is happening?" Alex asked herself as

she opened the box. She uncovered a mirror with a large crack running diagonally through it. The reflection was not Alex; it was the reflection of a young woman located in what appeared to be a college dorm room. The woman looked familiar.

"Jamie? Jamie Patterson?" Alex asked as her heart raced rapidly.

"Look out! She's right behind you!" Jamie yelled back at Alex. Alex turned around to see a woman with long hair covering her face. She wore a white gown and stared coldly at Alex from the open front door...

CHAPTER 4

t was 3:33 PM, and Dr. Yang grew increasingly concerned as he had not heard from Alex after he sent the text message in the morning. He left Mary to sort Dr. Collier's old files, which would take some time. So, he decided to pay Alex a visit.

"Alex, this is Paul," he said over the car's speaker phone. "I haven't heard from you. I am a bit worried. I am heading over to the guest house now. Please call me back as soon as you get this message."

Paul also tried to get in touch with Alex's boyfriend, but his phone went straight to voicemail. There was a massive wildfire that struck Southern California, and a number of firefighters in the San Francisco Bay Area were called in to help. Paul suspected that may be why Mike couldn't be reached.

As he pulled into the driveway, Paul saw Alex's car. This made him even more uncomfortable. Could Alex be incapacitated? He immediately ran out of his car and to the front door. The door was unlocked.

"Alex?! Alex, it's Paul!"

Paul entered the home to find items scattered all over the

living room; boxes were opened and the contents poured out as if *someone* entered the home with the intention of finding *something specific*. He then heard some rustling near one of the boxes.

Mee—row!!

"Good God!" Paul shouted as he placed his hand near is heart. It was Elmer, Alex's cat. Paul shook off the momentary scare. As Elmer darted off, something fell off the coffee table: it was a small package that was partially opened. Paul removed the rest of the packaging to uncover a Japanese doll dressed in a kimono.

"Odd…" Paul said in wonder. He placed the doll onto the coffee table when he noticed another peculiar object. It was a mirror with a large diagonal crack. The mirror's glass looked cloudy, so he could barely make out his own reflection. There was something written on the mirror in blood red: *Bring me Mary.* Paul gasped!

His phone buzzed. It was an unknown number. Breathing heavily, he proceeded to answer.

"Hello?" Paul asked in hesitation.

A muffled voice sounded on the other end. "Bring. Me. Mary."

"Who is this? What did you do to Alex?" Paul asked urgently.

"Upstairs bedroom," the voice muttered. The caller hung up.

Paul ran up the stairs to enter the top level where Alex resided. The bedroom door was slightly open. There was a foul odor coming from the bedroom. Paul opened the door and found Alex's lifeless body stretched out on the bed.

Paul closed his eyes, covered his mouth, and then turned his head briefly. Who could have done something like this? He opened his eyes and turned back to the horrific scene. Paul discovered that there was a message written on the wall near Alex's dreamcatcher, which hung directly above the bed's headboard. It appeared that the message was written using Alex's blood!

BRING ME MARY…

———

An hour had past, and Mary finally reached the bottom of the first box only to find a random thumb drive.

"Oh, God. Don't tell me that all these files were digitized…" Mary rolled her eyes as she picked up the device.

Mary walked over to the desk and sat down. She inserted the thumb drive into the laptop; the login credentials to the laptop were on a Post-It note attached next to the trackpad.

Mary opened the folder that appeared when the thumb drive loaded. There was one file with the name "SAC_052017.mp4." Mary opened the file. It was a movie — Dr. Scott Collier in a self-recording from a car at night.

My name is Dr. Scott Andrew Collier. I am a research scientist. It's Saturday, May 20, 2017 at 3:33 AM.

I think — I mean, I know I unleashed pure evil.

Scott sighed and looked away from the screen. Tears began to roll down his face.

I am a man of science. I wouldn't be saying any of this if I didn't witness it with my own eyes…

Back in March, I created a device that can record dreams. It was so amazing; I was able to watch everything that I dreamt the night before: vibrant colors; loved ones lost; exotic locations…

However, what I didn't notice until today was that the final scene of each recording contained a mirror in the background. And, in the mirror was a woman staring coldly at me. She had long, dark hair covering her face and wore a white gown. I believe this woman is known in the Eastern world as Hanako-san. In the West, she's known as Bloody Mary.

In the final recording from May 17th, she left a note on the mirror, written in blood. It said, "Bring me Mary."

Mary suddenly had a flashback to when she was 13 years old — to the day she saw a mysterious young girl with a teddy bear appear in the restroom mirror — and to the day she saw a woman in white at the cemetery. Mary went missing for a few weeks around the same time period; she could never recall what happened. The local Sheriff's department claimed that Mary was abducted by a cult that released her without any explanation. None of it added up, but Ross went along with the story. Mary had no reason *not* to believe Ross. Mary just assumed everyone was telling her the truth — *until now.*

Scott's video continued.

I have had no sleep. I lost my dreamcatcher the other night. But, I need to get back to my hotel. There's a lot more to discuss. I'll continue recording as I drive.

Scott started up the car, placed his phone on a mount, and began to drive. Before Scott could speak, there was a loud crash, and the video became jumbled. The recording ended.

"Oh my God!" Mary shouted. "This was the night Dr. Collier died! I need to talk to Paul."

Before Mary closed the file, she noticed something at the

end of the recording. She replayed the last scene before the crash and slowed down the frames. About 10 seconds before the crash, *there she was*. It was a woman with long, dark hair covering her face staring coldly at the screen.

"Bloody Mary!" Mary gasped. She grabbed her backpack and placed the thumb drive into one of the zip pouches. She ran from the small office to the elevator. The elevator stalled, so Mary rushed down the emergency staircase instead and found the main entrance. It was close to 6 PM; the receptionist was ready to leave for the day.

"Excuse me!" Mary shouted to the receptionist. "Where can I find Dr. Yang?"

The receptionist was a bit startled. "He went out to find Alex — Alex Anderson."

"Can I have the address?" Mary asked.

————

Mary drove to the address that the receptionist provided. There were a number of police cars and an ambulance. Mary parked along the street and jumped out of her car. She ran over to the front door but was stopped by the paramedics as they carted out a body from the house. She saw Paul inside talking to one of the paramedics. A young police officer proceeded to the front door, and Mary stopped her.

"May I ask what's going on?" Mary asked the officer.

"Are you a family member of the victim?" the officer asked.

Before Mary could answer, Paul appeared in the doorway and interjected. "Mary, you can't be here. Something terrible happened to Alex, but this is not the time to talk."

"But, Paul…" Mary pleaded. "It's about Dr. Collier — and *Bloody Mary*!" She took the thumb drive out of her backpack and showed it to Paul.

"Where did you find that?" Paul's face grew pale as he asked the question.

"I found it in a box marked *May 2017*. It was a recording from the night Dr. Collier died—"

"Mary, come with me." Paul grabbed Mary's arm and walked with her toward her car so they could have some privacy. "What's this talk about Scott and 'Bloody Mary?'"

"The thumb drive contains a recording from Dr. Collier the night he died. He said he unleashed 'pure evil.' And, Paul, I *saw her* — Bloody Mary. She was in the back seat of Dr. Collier's car—"

Before Mary could continue, a burly man, around 40 years old, approached Mary and Paul.

"Did I hear someone say 'Bloody Mary?'" the man asked.

Paul and Mary didn't know what to say. The man sensed hesitation so he introduced himself.

"I'm Adam. Adam Scott, Homicide Department." Detective Scott displayed his badge. "What are your names?"

"I am Dr. Paul Yang. I own this house. This is my company's newest intern, Mary Montgomery. She was scheduled to move into the house today."

"Wait, Mary Montgomery of Edenvale, Ohio?" Detective Scott said in shock.

"Umm, yes; how did you know that?" Mary asked with a confused look.

"I was a deputy assigned to your missing persons case," Detective Scott explained. "It's a long story, but I moved out here to the Bay Area as the money and benefits were *much better*. Besides, between us, I *cannot wait* to retire! I get a full pension!

"Anyway, enough of the small talk," Detective Scott continued in a serious tone. "Tell me what happened, Dr. Yang."

"Just call me Paul, please," Paul said and then explained the events that led to the discovery of Alex's body.

"I hadn't heard from Alex. She was one of the most reliable people I know. When I got to the house, it was a complete mess. I received a mysterious phone call from an unknown number that said, 'Bring me Mary.'"

Mary gasped!

"What is it?" Detective Scott asked urgently.

"Paul, that's what Dr. Collier said that was on the mirror. It said, 'Bring me Mary.'"

"Mirror, what mirror, Mary?" Paul asked.

"From Dr. Collier's dreams!" Mary added.

"Okay, let's back up here… Who is 'Dr. Collier?' And what about this 'mirror' and 'dream?'" Detective Scott was lost at this point.

Before Mary or Paul could answer, Henry, from Detective Scott's forensics team, ran from inside the house and interrupted the group's conversation. "Detective Scott! We have camera footage!"

Paul, Mary, Henry, and Detective Scott entered the house and walked to the kitchen table, where Henry had set up his equipment.

Henry sat down and guided the team through his discovery.

"Seems there was a doorbell camera installed. The username and password details were left behind on the kitchen countertop. It was set up to store recordings in the cloud. It only captured a few minutes, however, as the battery wasn't fully charged, and there was no audio."

Henry played the video clip. It showed Mike leaving the house and Alex closing the door.

"That's Mike, Alex's boyfriend," Paul confirmed.

Then, about three minutes later, 3:33 AM, it showed Alex opening the door and realizing that there was no one there. Alex walked back into the house and left the door open. Then, a figure walked up to the door. It was a woman wearing jeans and a sweatshirt. She had long, dark hair.

Detective Scott gasped!

"Who is that?" Paul asked.

"It's Jamie. Jamie Patterson..." Detective Scott replied in shock.

CHAPTER 5

Mark took a deep breath as he entered a conference room filled with some of the most brilliant minds in machine learning. It was his first week at Patterson AI, and the engineering managers were already impressed with Mark's ability to decipher complex algorithms. He was a problem solver and could always get to the root cause of an issue.

Shelly learned of Mark's joining the company and immediately buried all her ill-will. It was obvious to most that Shelly had a massive crush on Mark, ever since high school. Her loyalty to Jamie, however, kept her feelings in check. Now that Mark seemed to have moved on, Shelly felt that maybe it was her chance.

As soon as his meeting ended, Mark found Shelly waiting anxiously outside the conference room. He gave her a warm smile. It was nice to see his old friend again.

"Hey, wanna grab lunch today?" Shelly asked eagerly.

"Sure, Shell. Let me first catch up on some messages, and I'll join you in the cafeteria. Give me like, ten minutes."

Shelly nodded and headed out to the cafeteria.

Patterson AI had an open floorplan — no partitions; lots

of room for collaboration. It was a casual-dress environment and had a "Silicon Valley"-feel to it. There were game rooms, lounges with televisions, tons of snacks — a really great atmosphere. Many of the engineers were heads-down with noise-cancelling headphones. They were all so passionate about what they were trying to accomplish. Mark sat down at his desk space, which was equipped with four large interconnected monitors, transparent displays, and random robotic gadgets — the casual observer could equate it to comic book hero Tony Stark's lab.

The company had been in business for close to 30 years. It pivoted over the course of the last few years to focus heavily on personal assistant technology that could *relate* to you; a digital "best friend," if you will. The company went public in 2019. It had an unprecedented IPO, which gave Allan Patterson the funds to expand and invest in areas that interested him. As a result, Mr. Patterson created a top-secret division, PattersonX. He invested in a number of start-ups that focused on sleep and consciousness studies. Rumor had it that they were close to solving the "mind-body problem." Mr. Patterson's obsession in this area had been criticized by investors, but this was personal for him. He lost his daughter; if there was even a remote chance that consciousness continued beyond death, it would help him and his wife, Jenny, to cope.

Mark looked at his phone, and there were 15 messages from Pete Williams. The first message read:

We need to talk. Urgent.

How many times did Pete send a message like that since Jamie's disappearance? 100 times? Mark hit the "Block This Sender" button and deleted the remaining messages without reading them.

"It's time to start your new life," Mark thought to himself.

He placed his phone and laptop into his backpack and headed over to the cafeteria.

Mark grabbed a sandwich and soda and walked over to Shelly. Shelly wore an OSU hoodie and some jeans. She had her long, dark hair tied in a pony tail. Mark didn't realize until just now how pretty she was. She gave Mark the biggest smile as he sat down across from her at a small table.

"So how do you like it here so far?" Shelly asked between bites of her salad.

"Yeah, it's great!" Mark said with genuine enthusiasm. "The people are all very nice, and they are having me work on some really cool projects."

"That's awesome! You can see why people have been calling this place the *Midwest Google*." Shelly continued the small talk. "Are you going to work on your Bachelor's degree?"

"Yeah," Mark replied. "There is a fast track BS/MS program through OSU that I am looking into. I just need about six months here to get the education assistance for it. It's really great. I feel I can get back on track, you know."

"That's so awesome, Mark!" Shelly replied.

Shelly took a deep breath and then spoke gently: "I hope this isn't too personal, but how are you coping? I know a while back I kinda got angry at you—"

"No, it's okay, Shell," Mark interrupted. "You were right. All those 'wild goose chases' had to stop. *We* know who took Jamie, but she's been quiet for seven years. I can't put my life on hold anymore." Mark reached out and held Shelly's left hand. "I'm ready to move on. I think Jamie would have wanted that…"

Before Mark could continue, a man in a lab coat interrupted the moment. He wore a Patterson AI consultant badge. It was Dr. Paul Yang.

"Mark Stevens, I'm Dr. Paul Yang. I need to talk with you

— in private." He looked over at Shelly as he spoke the last word.

"Dr. Paul Yang, the parapsychologist?" Mark asked.

"Yes, Patterson AI is one of the main investors of my lab in Palo Alto, California. I am working on an initiative at PattersonX in which I need your assistance."

Mark looked at Shelly, and she gave him a shrug.

"Okay, let's grab a conference room," Mark said as he stood up and headed off with Paul.

———

Mark led Paul to a small, sound-proof phone room where they could talk in private and shut the door. There were two chairs and a small desk. Mark and Paul sat down and faced each other.

Before Paul could speak, Mark interjected firmly: "Look, I know you are friends with Pete Williams from *Things That Go Bump in the Night*. I already told Pete; I'm done. There have been hundreds of 'Jamie sightings' and none of them have panned out. Most people are looking for attention or a slice of the million dollar reward that Mr. Patterson posted—"

"My assistant was murdered!" Paul interrupted Mark.

"Oh my God! I'm so sorry," Mark replied earnestly.

Paul paused for a moment and replied: "Thank you. Her name was Alex. Alex Anderson."

"Wait," Mark interjected. "Wasn't Alex the person who encountered the man in the fedora in her dreams?"

"Yes, how did you know that?" Paul asked, eyebrows crunched.

"Pete..." Mark replied.

"Damnit!" Paul shouted. "He can't keep his big mouth shut. Fortunately, we were able to stop the dream monster. But, our bigger enemy — *SHE'S BACK*."

"How do you know?" Mark asked with skepticism.

"I know she murdered Alex." Paul reached into his lab coat pocket and handed Mark a Japanese doll. "Look at the doll's tag." The following characters were printed on the tag: 花子さんの財産.

"It's in Japanese, but I recognize these characters: *Property of Hanako-San*," Mark said.

"Yes," Paul said. "I found this doll among all the packages in the living room."

"Isn't that crime scene evidence?" Mark inquired.

"Yes, but I didn't want it bagged up and lost. It may help us — along with this." Paul took out his phone and showed Mark a photo of the long mirror with the diagonal crack.

"That's the mirror from Jamie and Shelly's dorm room! How did you find it?" Mark asked anxiously.

"It's a long story, Mark. But, look closer." Paul zoomed in on the image to show Mark the words in blood red: "Bring Me Mary."

"Mary?" Mark asked.

"Yes, I think she's looking for Mary Montgomery," Paul replied.

"Little Mary? Well, I guess she's, what, 21 now?"

"Yes, she's an intern at my lab! She moved to California in 2018 and is a psychology prodigy. I need your help to understand why she's being targeted."

"Paul, there are a lot of people named 'Mary.' How do we know it's Mary Montgomery that she's after?"

"I don't. But that's why I need your help…"

Mark paused and then shook his head. "No, Paul. I can't. I'm picking up the pieces, moving on with my life…"

"No one has to know, Mark." Paul softened his tone. "I'm recruiting you for PattersonX! Allan has given me free rein to involve anyone I want in the mind-body problem project."

Mark sighed and then asked: "Well, what does this have to do with Jamie?"

"Take a look at this video. It was recorded at the house I

own in Palo Alto. I have researchers live here as a company perk." Paul opened the video doorbell footage from his phone. He fast-forwarded to the scene where the woman appeared at the door.

"Oh my God, that is Jamie!" Mark gasped. "But, we saw this before; back when Shelly saw 'The Woman in White' in the dorm room..."

"Exactly," Paul agreed. "My suspicion is that Hanako-san 'appears' as Jamie on video. She's doing this to fool us."

"Well, what are the authorities saying?" Mark asked. "And, did anyone tell the Pattersons?"

"The authorities are baffled. They want to bring in the woman from the video for questioning. There is no direct evidence — no finger prints — nothing showing 'Jamie' did anything. Given how many 'Jamie sightings' there have been over the last seven years, the Detective does not want to say anything to the Pattersons until they know *for sure*. By the way, guess who is the lead on this case? Adam Scott, from the Mary Montgomery disappearance! You see how this is all adding up?"

Mark sighed.

"Look, Mark. I know you are trying to move on. I do respect that, believe it or not. I have a 4-bedroom apartment here in Columbus. I hid the mirror and the doll in my car before I called the police and quickly had them shipped here. So the police don't know anything about the mirror or the doll. I bought a plane ticket for Mary Montgomery to come out here as well. You don't have to travel. *No one has to know anything...*"

————

"Mark!" Shelly yelled as she saw Mark leave the phone room with Paul. "Have a moment?"

"I'll see you later, Mark." Paul nodded at Mark and left him to talk to his friend.

"Hey, what's up?" Mark asked with a small sigh.

"Oh, umm. Is everything okay?" Shelly didn't want to be nosy, but she was always the "queen of gossip" — ever since grade school.

"All good! Um, Paul wants me to join his 'mind-body problem' project. It's actually really awesome! Unfortunately, I am under a strict NDA. He wanted to go over that and have me sign it."

Shelly knew Mark well enough to tell when he was stretching the truth, but she didn't want to create any tension, especially since there was a hint that Mark may be interested in her beyond friendship.

"Okay. Well, I was wondering... a group of us are going out for some drinks after work. Wanna join us?" Shelly asked hopefully.

"Oh, I am so sorry; Paul wants to get started ASAP. Can I take a rain check?"

Mark saw the disappointment on Shelly's face. He reached over to her and gave her a hug.

"Hey, I'll see you on Monday. We'll have lunch, for sure. And, if I can squeeze in some time next weekend, would you like to see a movie?"

Shelly's mood changed immediately. "Yes! I would love that."

"Okay! Think about what you want to see. See you Monday." Mark walked away from Shelly and immediately turned his focus to everything Paul discussed. "Bloody Mary," Mark thought. "We are going to silence you — *for good*!"

CHAPTER 6

"You are going *where*?" Ross Montgomery gave Mary a stern look as she began packing.

"Dr. Yang needs me to go to Columbus for a project with PattersonX. We may have a breakthrough with the 'mind-body problem.'" Mary stretched the truth a bit as she didn't want her dad worrying.

"But, Mary, *Alex Anderson was murdered*. She was murdered in the house *you* were going to stay at. I mean, what if you are in danger, too?" Ross sat down on Mary's bed as he watched her pack.

Mary paused for a moment. It was finally time to get the truth from Ross.

"Maybe I am in danger, Dad?" Mary stated boldly. "Maybe 'Bloody Mary' wants to capture me *again*…?"

Ross was taken aback by the statement. "What? What are you talking about, Mary?"

"You heard me, Dad. I was missing for two weeks. I wasn't taken by a 'cult' was I?" Mary's eyes began to water. "I need to know the *truth*." Mary sat next to Ross and held his hands.

"Okay, Mary. You are an adult now. Maybe it's time I tell

you. Yes, on May 20, 2017, you went missing. We uncovered, with the help of the local Sheriff's office and two teens, that you had been abducted by Hanako-san, also known as 'Bloody Mary.' I can't believe I am actually saying this — she was an urban legend, but I guess some legends are grounded in the truth. There appears to be some portal. Apparently, the man you hold in such high regard, Dr. Scott Collier, may have opened this portal by mistake in March of 2017, two months before your disappearance. Scientists have theorized for centuries that there is some 'multiverse.' But now we know it's real — all of it."

Ross paused for a moment, as he had been rehearsing this in his mind for years, and it was such a relief to get it off his chest.

"When you were gone for the two weeks, you were in another dimension. Time, as you know it here on this Earth, did not exist there. From your perspective, you were gone for a split second.

"The Sheriff's department felt it necessary to keep this under wraps. If word got out, it would change the course of humanity. They didn't feel people were ready for this revelation, so it was best to stay silent and make up the story about the cult."

Mary hugged Ross. "Thank you, Dad, for being honest with me. I still don't remember anything that happened when I was in this other dimension. In a way, that may be a blessing in disguise. Who knows what Hanako-san had in store for me?" Mary shivered thinking about it.

"Don't worry, Dad. I promise to stay safe while I am away. I'll leave you my address and will have my phone with me at all times." Mary gave her dad one more hug.

"You have a good head on your shoulders, and I *trust you*." Ross let out a sigh. "But, please, Mary, come back home safely."

———

Ross dropped Mary off at San Francisco International Airport. It was crowded as always, but Paul upgraded Mary to First Class as a gesture of gratitude. As a result, she was able to make her way through security quickly. Mary parked herself at a table where she could use her laptop as she waited for her boarding group to be called.

As she waited at the gate, Mary couldn't help but notice a peculiar-looking man who seemed to be watching her. He was Caucasian, average height, and had thick gray hair. He wore a dark turtleneck shirt and gray slacks. He sat at one of the chairs facing Mary's table. The man looked down at his phone and periodically glanced over at Mary.

Mary wasn't sure what to think at this point. Was he just some creepy old guy? But, oddly enough, he seemed somewhat familiar…

"At least I'm in a public place," Mary reconciled to herself.

She put on her headphones and attempted to block him from her mind. About ten minutes had passed, and Mary garnered some courage to look over to where the man was sitting — but he was gone!

"First Class passengers, get ready to board." The announcer called out Mary's boarding group. She quickly gathered up her things and headed to the line. Periodically, Mary turned her head and looked around, but there was no sign of the stranger.

Mary sat in her assigned seat by the window, and the other passengers followed suit. She couldn't help but wonder if the mystery man would be on her flight. The seat next to Mary remained empty.

"Miss, I'm Leya. What would you like to drink?" A tall, thin woman of African descent, possibly in her 30s, serviced the First Class cabin. She held a pen and notepad as she questioned Mary.

"Just water, please," Mary said calmly. "Um, Leya, I hope you don't mind me asking, but is the seat next to me going to be occupied?"

Before Leya could answer the question, the cabin lavatory door opened, and the stranger walked out and headed over to the seat next to Mary!

"Do you want your usual, Mr. Williams?" Leya asked as she gave a warm smile to the stranger.

"Yes, and, please… just call me Pete." The man stashed his carry-on bag in the upper bin while addressing the stewardess.

Once Mary heard his voice, she was able to put it all together.

"Oh my God! You're Pete Williams from *Things That Go Bump in the Night*!" Mary squealed.

"Right… and you're Mary Montgomery," Pete said, as he settled into his seat.

"Wait, you know who I am?" Mary asked in a hesitant tone.

"Well, you may have noticed that I kept looking at you; I knew you were heading to Columbus, but I wasn't sure if you were the same 'Mary Montgomery from Edenvale.' You look a lot different." Pete gave Mary a reassuring smile.

"Oh, yeah, my 'awkward years.'" Mary rolled her eyes. "But, how did you get on this plane? I didn't even see you board. And, how did you know I would be on this flight?" Mary looked inquisitively at Pete.

"Geez, lots of questions. I like it!" Pete smiled. "I pre-boarded; part of the Million Mile Club. Been doing a lot of travel over the last seven years. Paul Yang invited me; he told me you would be on this flight."

"Oh, I see," Mary said in realization. "Well, what does Paul want from you?"

Pete hesitated but lent an answer. "It's time to stop *her*, once and for all. And, I think we finally know how to do it."

Leya arrived with Pete's drink and Mary's bottle of water.

"Here's your Bloody Mary, Pete," Leya said with a smile. Mary looked at Pete in amusement.

"And here's your water, Miss."

"Wait." Pete grabbed the water bottle and turned to Mary. "You're 21 now, right? This is a long flight. Leya, can we get a *real* drink for Miss Montgomery?" Pete winked at Mary. Leya obliged and handed Mary a blood-red concoction.

"Water..." Pete rolled his eyes jokingly. "To the devil with false modesty." Pete held his drink to Mary for a toast.

Mary laughed while toasting: "To the devil!"

Mary coughed as she sipped the strong beverage. "Um, can I just stick with water?" Mary asked as she continued to cough. Pete let out a laugh.

———

Over the course of the flight, Pete briefed Mary on the search for Jamie — seven years of dead-end leads. "I was ready to give up on the search," Pete explained, "but then I heard from Paul. Terrible what happened to Alex, but this is the break we've been looking for."

"Pete, did Paul tell you about Dr. Collier's video?" Mary asked.

"Woah, *what video*?" Pete asked in shock.

Mary grabbed her backpack and pulled out the thumb drive, headphones, and laptop. She inserted the thumb drive into the laptop and loaded the video. Mary handed her laptop and headphones to Pete.

Pete watched the video in dismay. *"Bring me Mary?"* Pete questioned as he took off the headphones.

"Yes!" Mary shouted. "But, that's not everything. Slow down the last 10 seconds, and tell me what you see."

Paul followed Mary's instructions and only saw static. "I don't see anything, Mary."

"What?!" Mary asked anxiously. She grabbed the laptop from Pete. "It should be right... here...?" Mary looked shocked as there was nothing but static...

CHAPTER 7

Paul invited Mark to his high-rise apartment in downtown Columbus. Although Mark agreed to assist, he resolved that this would be the *last time*. Mark's future looked bright — a great gig at Patterson AI; a chance to further develop his relationship with Shelly — as much as he loved Jamie, it was time to close this case *for good*.

Mark took the elevator up to the twelfth floor. Classical music played as multiple people made their way on and off. Mark finally reached the top floor. He walked over to apartment 1287 and rang the doorbell.

A familiar young woman opened the door. "Mark! It's been forever!" Mary Montgomery greeted Mark with a warm smile. "Come on in."

"Mary? Mary Montgomery? Wow!" As he entered the apartment, Mark was taken aback by how different Mary appeared from when he last saw her: she was radiant and confident.

"Yeah, I know: I get that reaction a lot from people who knew me during my 'awkward phase...'" Mary let out a sigh but stayed in good spirits.

"You look amazing," Mark said as he hugged Mary. "And

congratulations on your academic success. Ross must be so proud."

"Thanks, Mark! Yes, he certainly is." Mary paused for a moment. Mark was like a brother she never had. They stayed in touch periodically after Mary was rescued. "We can catch up more later; the team is anxious to get started. Let's head to the war room."

"*War room*? Okay..." Mark furrowed his eyebrows as he followed Mary to a large room which looked like something out of a crime scene investigation: a map with pins and strings that connected points A to B; photos of Jamie, Alex, Paul's house, and Jamie's dorm room pinned to cork boards; the Japanese doll sat on the coffee table; and the mirror with the diagonal crack rested against one of the walls. While sitting on a luxurious sofa, two men discussed something softly while enjoying glasses of wine. The gray haired gentleman noticed Mark and Mary enter the room.

"Look who's here; the man who blocks my messages," Pete Williams said sarcastically as he stood up from the couch while still holding his wine glass.

"Okay, Pete..." Mark said hesitantly.

"Hahaha!" Pete laughed as he placed his wine glass on the table. "Give me a hug, bro!"

Mark rolled his eyes and hugged Pete in hesitation.

"Glad to have you back, man!" Pete shouted.

"I'm not 'back,' Pete," Mark said firmly. "As I told Paul, this is it. *One last time*..." Mark looked over to the other man on the couch as he spoke the words.

Paul stood up from the couch.

"Glad you came over, Mark," Paul said as he shook Mark's hand.

"Please, have a seat." Paul motioned to Mark to have a seat on the sofa. "Would you like a glass of wine?" Paul offered to Mark. Mark politely declined.

"Mary has an important video to show us," Paul said as

he looked over at Mary. "I haven't seen it yet, but both Mary and Pete have."

Mary connected her laptop to the 70-inch wall mount television in the war room. "To give you some context, Mark," Mary interjected, "we are about to show you a video from Dr. Scott Collier: the night of his death."

"How were you able to get a hold of that?" Mark asked as he sat on one of the couches in the room.

"I found it in a box back at Paul's lab in Palo Alto," Mary said. "Brace yourself; it's disturbing."

Mary loaded the video, and Mark and Paul watched as Dr. Collier explained the portal, unleashing evil, and the connection to Bloody Mary.

When the end of the video loaded, Mark noticed something odd. "Wait! There was something in the last frame. Can you rewind, Mary?"

"Yeah! I thought I saw something, too, but it wasn't there when I showed this video to Pete on the airplane."

Mary slowed down the last few seconds, but this time it wasn't Bloody Mary…

"My God, that's Jamie!" Pete's jaw dropped. "Looks like she's saying something. Can we make it out?"

"I think she just said, 'Help!'" Paul said hesitantly.

Mary paused the video. "Wait! When I was at Paul's lab, I saw Bloody Mary in this final frame. She said, 'Bring me Mary.' And now, we are seeing Jamie Patterson asking for help?! *What does Bloody Mary want? What the hell is going on?* None of this makes sense!"

"Actually, it does. It makes perfect sense." A portly man with a gray beard entered the room. He wore a buttoned shirt and tan slacks. He slowly removed the hat from his head.

"Sheriff King?!" Mark shouted in amazement.

The Sheriff acknowledged Mark with a friendly nod.

"The 'Redneck Fox Mulder' is back! I thought you weren't

allowed to help us with Jamie's disappearance?" Pete asked curiously.

"Yes, and no. As of today, I am no longer 'Sheriff King.' You can now call me 'Detective King.' I retired from Waverly County and now work as a private investigator. An old friend, Detective Adam Scott, gave me a call and said you all were stuck. So, Paul here told me about this meeting place, gave me an entrance code, and here I am."

"Well, welcome to the investigation, *Detective* King," Mary said with a smile. "So why does all this make sense to you?"

"Kids, let's all sit down and get comfortable. It's time to go back to May 20, 1904 — the night *Mary Hunter* disappeared…"

CHAPTER 8

Edenvale, Ohio
May 20, 1904

"You go up to the attic right now, young lady!" Mary Hunter was sound asleep when her mother yelled at her. Rosa Hunter Patterson had a difficult time sleeping, which was usually the case when her husband, Elias, was up late working. Rosa went into the kitchen and noticed her favorite tea cup was broken. She assumed it was Mary's fault, as Mary had been swinging her new doll around the kitchen that evening. The doll was a gift from Elias. He found the doll one day when he was cleaning the attic. It was exquisite — dressed in a kimono; it was most likely hand-crafted in Japan. He cleaned it up and gave it to Mary for her 13th birthday.

"I call her 'Little Mary,'" Elias mused as he handed the doll to his stepdaughter.

"I love it!" Mary said enthusiastically and hugged Elias. Rosa watched from the kitchen while the two were celebrating. Rosa was angered each time she saw Elias grow fonder of Mary — some sort of deep-rooted jealousy and fear.

"No! I don't want to go up there, Mother! It's scary!" Mary screamed back at Rosa.

Rosa grabbed Mary by the arm and dragged her out of bed. Mary held onto her doll as tight as she could while Rosa forced Mary down the hall and up the stairway. Rosa knew that Mary had a fear of the attic. In fact, Mary stated that she felt something or *someone* was watching her in the old garret, ever since she and her friends played "an old children's game" up there.

They reached the attic door. Mary tried hard to resist, but Rosa was able to lock Mary into the room.

"No, Mother, no!" Mary screamed in terror while facing the door. Mary was in tears and turned around slowly only to see the mirror right in front of her! Instead of Mary's reflection, she saw a *woman inside the mirror*! The woman had long, dark hair covering her face and wore a white gown. The woman's hand stretched out from inside the mirror to grab Mary! Mary screamed!

"Mary?" Rosa asked. "What's going on in there?" She was unable to open the door.

It was 3:33 AM, and Elias was in his outdoor workshop. He heard the commotion; in fact, even the neighbors heard the screams and joined Elias as they stormed into the house.

"Rosa?! Mary?!" Elias yelled.

"Help!" Rosa screamed out loud. Elias and his neighbors followed the sound to the upstairs attic. When they arrived, the attic door was open, and Rosa stood there in front of the mirror while holding "Little Mary" in her hands.

"Mary — Mary's gone! *She* took her!" Rosa explained as her face turned ghostly white...

CHAPTER 9

"So, 'Bring me Mary' really means 'Bring me the doll?'" Mary Montgomery asked.

"Exactly," Detective King said as he took the Japanese doll from the coffee table and made himself comfortable on the sofa. "Hanako-san wanted Mary's doll. There were a series of these dolls made; hand-crafted in Osaka, Japan. They were Hanako-san's playthings: Muffy, Buffy, Duffy, and this one. We don't have a name for it, other than *Little Mary*. It serves as a talisman. With it, Bloody Mary can jump to *any portal* in *any dimension — on any Earth — without being summoned*.

"Wait, you are talking about the multiverse," Mary said surprisingly. "So *it is* true."

"Welcome to the club, Mary," Paul said with a smile. "Scott and I hypothesized about this for years..."

"Yes, young Mary," Detective King interjected. "Ross called this morning and told me that he revealed the *real* reason why you went missing years ago. I don't know if you ever heard the term *ontological shock*? Well, we were afraid that most people would not be able to handle the truth; hence, the 'cult' cover story."

"It's been a lot to absorb," Mary asserted, "but I *needed* to know the truth — especially now."

"Understood, Miss Mary." Detective King let out a sigh.

"To continue with the doll... This specific doll became the talisman, as it was there with Hanako-san the day she was *murdered*. She was found dead in her school's restroom on the 3rd floor in stall number 3 on the 3rd day of the month..."

"Three thirty-three: the Witching Hour," Pete affirmed.

"Do we know what happened to the other dolls?" Mary asked.

"I know the answer," Pete said. "I have had reports on my show about mischievous Japanese dolls that have resulted in disappearances or possibly *murder*."

"Ugh, how creepy!" Mary shivered.

"Mary, don't go down that rabbit hole." Mark shoved his right elbow into Pete.

"Ow!" Pete pouted at Mark.

"Okay — I have a *real* question for you, Detective King," Mark said as he gave Pete an annoyed look. "Where has she been over the last seven years? Pete and I have been on so many wild goose chases, but we haven't seen Bloody Mary."

"I'm trying to figure that out as well," Detective King answered. "I suspect this mirror holds the clue." The detective pointed at the large mirror that was once in Jamie and Shelly's dorm room. "Where did you all find it?"

"Well, I can answer that one," Paul declared to the group. "We had a visiting scholar from Ohio State for a few months. She brought over a number of items that she was researching. Her interest was in the occult. I was a bit hesitant, but I let her bring over what she needed for her research. I had no idea that she was in possession of this specific mirror and the doll. She headed to Tahoe over winter break and died in a tragic ski accident. Her family only requested a few things to be returned. Alex was tasked with going through the remaining items and scheduling junk pickup or donation. I had no clue as to how she obtained the items. I asked her assistants and colleagues, but no one seemed to have any information.

"Detective King," Paul continued, "why did Alex have to die? What made Bloody Mary want her dead?"

"That is also a mystery. But, folks, we may be able to get our answer soon. Did you all get enough sleep? I have a feeling we'll have a friend appear in that mirror over yonder at 3:33 AM!"

"Jamie?" Mark asked.

"Yes, young Mark. When you all heard Miss Jamie say '*Help*,' she's actually saying she wants to help *us*…"

———

Mary, Paul, and Pete decided to take quick naps, while Detective King and Mark continued to talk.

"Why this specific mirror, Detective King? I thought the main portal was in Beth Reese's room — the one that was in the Patterson family for years and even took Mary Hunter?"

"Young Mark, do you know if Bloody Mary has been summoned prior on *this mirror*?"

"Oh no!" Mark realized. "Shelly's graduation party. Jamie was in the bathroom and a group of us played the Bloody Mary game. Oh, God, it's all our fault!"

"Don't blame yourself, young Mark. You didn't know. We'll get to the bottom of it."

———

It was 3:33 AM, and the group gathered around the mirror.

"What can we expect?" Paul asked Detective King after stretching and letting out a yawn.

"Soon we should have a glimpse into where Jamie has been captured. Let's hope she's there and in a safe space to talk with us."

As Detective King finished his sentence, the mirror changed from being a reflection of the war room to a window into Jamie's dorm room. It appeared almost exactly how she and Shelly decorated it.

"Hello? Miss Jamie?" Detective King asked the mirror.

"Sheriff King?" A young woman's voice called out. "Is that you?"

"Yes, yes it is. I go by Detective King now. Is that you, Miss Jamie?"

Suddenly, in front of the mirror, Jamie Patterson appeared. Mark recognized her immediately; she was wearing the exact same outfit she wore on their final video call that fateful day in October 2017. She was as beautiful as ever.

"Jamie! I'm here, too!" Mark couldn't help but reach out.

"Mark! Mark!" Jamie yelled. "I can't see you. The mirror is foggy. I can hear you and Detective King! Who all is there with you?"

"Miss Jamie, we have myself, Mark, Mary Montgomery, Pete Williams from *Things That Go Bump in the Night*, and Dr. Paul Yang, a parapsychologist. We are all here to help."

"I don't have much time. I don't know when she's going to come back. I know you all probably have tons of questions, and I want to help!" Jamie shouted back to the team behind the foggy mirror.

"Yes, we do have some questions. First, Jamie, are you hurt or injured?" Detective King asked.

"I am not hurt. In fact, The Woman in White — I've been told to not use the *other* name — *needs me alive*. When traveling outside the mirror, she has to project as someone in human form. I agreed for her to use me if it meant protecting all of you."

"That's probably why she's been silent for over the last seven years," Pete declared.

"Seven years?" Jamie asked. "I feel as if I have only been here a few hours."

"Yes, Jamie," Pete interjected. "Time, as we know it here on Earth, is a construct that may not exist in your new reality."

"Jamie, you said that we would be protected. Well, then why was Alex Anderson murdered?" Paul's voice trembled as he asked the question.

"The Woman in White made a deal with some shadowy figure. A man who wears a fedora…"

"Oh my God!" Pete said as he and Paul looked at each other. "The man who haunts people in their sleep…"

"He wanted her to obtain Alex's dreamcatcher so he could take her soul in her sleep. In exchange, he promised to lead her to a Japanese doll. It's a special doll she had as a child. He told her it was located in the house in which Alex was staying. The Woman in White can only stay in human form for a short period of time. She searched frantically but was not able to locate it. Enraged, she didn't complete her deal with the man in the fedora. Instead, she sought revenge: *The Woman in White murdered Alex*." Jamie let out a big sigh.

"I am so sorry for your loss. She seemed like a wonderful person," Jamie said with deep sympathy.

"Thank you, Jamie," Paul replied.

"Well, Miss Jamie, we acquired the doll. However, The Woman in White stayed long enough to use your image on camera. The police are suspecting *you* in the murder of Alex Anderson."

"I guess it serves me right for making a deal with the devil," Jamie said quietly.

"No, don't blame yourself," Mark consoled Jamie. "Look, this may actually all be *my fault*…" Mark confessed.

"No, young Mark," Detective King attempted to stop him.

"No, she needs to hear this," Mark demanded.

"Hear what, Mark?" Jamie asked with concern.

"The night of the graduation party — at Shelly's — when you went to the bathroom, a group of us played the game. We summoned The Woman in White through this very mirror. This is all my fault."

"No, Mark," Jamie replied with deep concern. "It's not your fault. You couldn't have known. *This woman is evil.* She finds a way to get what she wants."

"Jamie, it's Mary Montgomery. I am forever grateful for you, Mark, and Detective King for all your help in my safe return. I owe you so much, Jamie. What can I do to help?"

"That's very sweet, Mary," Jamie replied. "But I think there is only one way to end this. Please, hand me the doll so I can destroy it. And then close this portal for good."

"There has to be another way, Jamie," Pete argued.

"Actually, Miss Jamie is right," Detective King countered. "Destroying the talisman in Hanako-san's home dimension should break the curse and will render her powerless. Jamie can still survive in this alternative reality. Bringing her back to *our reality* will just cause—"

"*Ontological shock,*" Mary replied.

"Exactly." Detective King nodded.

Mark moved close to the mirror. "Jamie, you know I will always love you. I understand what you have to do. There was not a single day that went by when I didn't think about you. But knowing that you will be safe, even though we will be apart, will make me happy."

"Mark, my love, I want you to be happy, too. You have a great support system there. It's my time to do something greater than myself. Be sure to tell my parents that I love them."

Jamie reached her hand through the mirror. Tearfully, Detective King handed the doll to Jamie.

"When I shout out to you, crush this mirror immediately!" Jamie demanded. "She's going to come back here soon; she will be able to sense that I have the doll. Get ready."

Paul had several sledgehammers ready, as he suspected that at some point the mirror would need to be destroyed. He,

Pete, and Mark stood on guard as they waited for Jamie's signal.

———

Jamie waited patiently in her room, as she listened for Bloody Mary. She opened the dorm room door and the hallway lights began to flicker. A shadowy figure proceeded down the hallway. It began moaning. It was The Woman in White.

"Bring. Me. Mary." Bloody Mary began to chant while also growling. "Bring. Me. Mary!"

Jamie shivered but stood her ground. "Come and get her!"

Jamie ran back into her room and stood on top of her desk. As Bloody Mary entered, Jamie had one hand on the doll's head and the other ready to rip it off its body.

"Not my Mary!" The Woman in White shrieked.

"Yes, it's time to die, bitch!"

Jamie ripped the doll apart and yelled to the mirror. "Destroy it now!"

Paul, Pete, and Mark heard Jamie's signal and immediately smashed the mirror.

Bloody Mary moaned in pain and tried to reach over to Jamie, but she crumbled to the ground. Her body began to wither, and then there was nothing left but the white gown.

"Finally, it's over," Jamie sighed.

CHAPTER 10

Oakridge Memorial Park
San Jose, California

"Alex Anderson was more than a friend. She was the most giving person I had ever met…" Steph tried hard to hold back her tears as she gave the eulogy. It took place not too far from where Alex's parents were interred. In fact, not too far from the crypt of Dr. Scott Collier…

"This isn't the most enjoyable place for a first date, but I am glad you were able to make it out here to California." Mark held Shelly's hand as they sat and listened to Steph's memorial to Alex.

"It's okay, Mark. And thank you for telling me everything that happened. I think we are starting off on the right foot." Shelly smiled and rested her head on Mark's right shoulder.

Paul, Pete, Mary and Ross Montgomery, Alex's boyfriend Mike, Steph's boyfriend Ryan, and Alex's sister were all in attendance. There were a number of others who attended: former colleagues, Ed from the thrift store that Alex frequented, and a young, beautiful woman wearing a large hat.

Once the service concluded, a few of the guests gathered around the garden near the mausoleum to catch up and have some drinks and light snacks.

"Hey, Paul, did you take Alex's dreamcatcher?" Pete whispered into Paul's ear and then sipped a glass of wine.

"I picked it up from Detective Scott before the memorial service." Paul patted his blazer pocket to indicate that the dreamcatcher was safe and sound.

Although it was a beautiful day in San Jose, it was quite windy. The napkins on the snack table began to fly away.

"I'll grab them!" Paul yelled as he attempted to rescue the napkins. As he turned, he accidentally bumped into the woman in the large hat. She had the most piercing green eyes. It caught Paul off-guard.

"Excuse me, Miss," Paul said politely.

"It's okay. A bit crowded. I was just leaving."

"Well, thanks for coming." Paul watched as the stunning woman left for her ride share, a red Tesla Model X.

"Wowza! Who was *that*?" Pete asked Paul as they watched the Tesla leave the memorial park.

"I have no idea. I think Mary was in charge of the guest list."

Paul walked over to Mary and asked, "Hey, who was that woman in the large hat?"

"Oh, let me check." Mary unlocked her tablet to browse the list. "I think her name was 'Genevieve.'"

"What?!" Paul yelled.

"Oh shit. Check your jacket pocket!" Pete urged.

"It's gone. The dreamcatcher is gone…"

I t seemed like just another day at Patterson AI. Allan Patterson was in the office to get the latest revenue forecast from the Finance team. While he waited, he received a page from his assistant.

"Mr. Patterson, you have a visitor: Detective King."

"Detective King?" Mr. Patterson was puzzled.

"Yes, he said you may know him as *Sheriff* Andy King of Waverly County. He investigated *Miss Jamie*'s accident seven years ago?"

"Ah, yes, please send him to my office."

Mr. Patterson stood up from his desk as he watched his assistant guide Detective King. He opened his office door and greeted the Detective.

"*Detective* King; did they demote you?!" Mr. Patterson said with a laugh.

"Nope, no demotion here. I retired from the Sheriff's Department and now work as a private investigator." Detective King answered as he walked into the office.

"Nice! So, to what do I owe this pleasure? Please have a seat. Would you like some coffee?"

"Oh no thank you, Mr. Patterson. This will be a short visit."

"Okay then, but call me Allan," Allan said with a smile. "Janet, please close the door on your way out."

Allan's assistant closed the door behind the detective.

"I don't know how to say this, but I will be direct. Miss Jamie is alive," Detective King said earnestly.

"What now? She is?! Where? Where is she? Have you seen her?" Allan shot out of his chair in an anxious joy.

"Mr. Allan. There is a lot more. Please, sit."

"Okay. If she's alive, that's great news, *isn't it*?" Allan questioned the detective.

Instead of answering the question, Detective King posed his own question. "Have you heard the term *ontological shock*?"

EPILOGUE

From the Journal of Jamie Patterson

I am trapped in this place that looks like Earth but doesn't feel the same. I am now Jamie Patterson of this new dimension. I am starting to remember things about this specific existence. My parents are Allan and Jenny Patterson, but Jenny died when I was born. I have a stepmother; her name is Janet. Allan doesn't have a robotics company; instead, he's a school teacher. Janet is a writer.

Shelly is still my roommate, but she only knows THIS version of "Jamie." Apparently, Shelly is very shy and would prefer to stay indoors. Quite the contrast from the OTHER Shelly who couldn't wait to pledge with the Tri-Delts… Her boyfriend is Steve. Yeah, Steve the "plus one."

The memories of my old life have been fading fast. I think I may have had a boyfriend. I remember that he was really smart, and I think he went to school in California. I can't really ask Shelly; she'll think it's weird that I don't remember my current life. The yearbooks are helping a bit. I guess I don't have a boyfriend? Oh well.

I'll take this journal with me as I head over to Starbucks (they still exist here; thank God!).

I walked over to the campus Starbucks. The young man who took my order was very nice. His name tag said his name was "Mark." He was tall and had sky blue eyes...

ABOUT THE AUTHOR

Growing up loving horror and mystery tales, JC Bratton writes short stories that pay homage to the Point Horror novels she would read as a kid: stories such as *Slumber Party* by Christopher Pike and *Twisted* by RL Stine. Some of her biggest influences are Alfred Hitchcock, Lois Duncan, Stephen King, and Richard Matheson.

JC hasn't given up on that Netflix movie deal! She resides in San Jose, California with her husband, stepsons, and cats.

ALSO FROM BLUE MILK PUBLISHING

Blue Milk Publishing represents independent authors of both fiction and non-fiction works.

*Please visit **bluemilk.co** for more information.*

Non-Fiction

The Cheating Boyfriend (And Other Organizational Indiscretions) (January 2017) by Jenny Hayes Carhart, MSOD, PHR

Fiction

Who's at the Door? (January 2020) by JC Bratton

Parasomnia (June 2020) by JC Bratton

Dollhouse (October 2020) by JC Bratton

Things That Go Bump in the Night (November 2020) by JC Bratton

Who's Back at the Door? (October 2023) by JC Bratton